Prince BJ
and
Princess Patch
Save their friends from the Wildfire

ISBN 979-8-88851-563-1 (Paperback)
ISBN 979-8-88851-564-8 (Digital)

Covenant Books
11661 Hwy 707
Murrells Inlet, SC 29576
www.covenantbooks.com

Prince BJ
and
Princess Patch

Save their friends from the Wildfire

D. Lindsay

One day Prince BJ was outside bringing in firewood for the fireplace. Princess Patch was inside doing her nails. Prince BJ asked Princess Patch, "Let's sleep outside in the tent tonight. Well, what do you say?"

Princess Patch said, "That sounds like fun."

So the puppies spent all morning getting their gear ready and their tent. Mom packed them snacks and told them, "Please be very careful and come in if you get scared."

Off they went to put up their tent. Princess Patch said, "This is too much work. I need a break."

Prince BJ said, "Thanks, sis." So Prince BJ asked Willow and Lily if they would help.

Willow said, "Of course, Prince BJ. This is what we are here for, to help you royal puppies."

It started getting dark, and they had their lantern on, and they were eating their snacks. The temperature dropped, and they had to put on something warmer. They cuddled up and went to sleep.

They were awoken by the sounds of the forest crackling. They got up and stepped out of the tent, and there from afar was a wildfire raging. There was a chill in the air. As they started walking deeper into the forest, it became warmer, so they knew they were getting closer.

When they reached the wildfire, the rangers were keeping it in control. The rangers said to the puppies, "You must stay back so you don't get hurt."

Prince BJ said, "I want to help."

Princess Patch said, "Can I help too?"

The rangers said, "Okay, but you have to put on a fire suit."

The puppies said, "This is going to be so much fun. We get to help." They had their suits on, and they were hot.

Princess Patch said, "Do you feel that?"

"What is it?" asked Prince BJ.

Princess Patch said, "Mosquitoes. Lots of them."

Prince BJ said, "Yes I feel them there swarming around us."

"Run the other way," said Princess Patch.

After losing the mosquitos, the puppies got back to the rangers. Everyone was talking. Prince BJ tried to hear what they were talking about.

Princess Patch asked, "What is it? what's wrong?"

"I don't know, Princess Patch. No one will talk to me," said Prince BJ.

Princess Patch walked over to the crowd slowly and quietly. She overheard that a puppy was in trouble, not just any puppy but Sophia. "Sophia is a friend of ours. I have to tell Prince BJ. Prince BJ fancies Sophia."

Princess Patch said, "Prince BJ, please sit down a minute. I have something to tell you.

Prince BJ asked, "What is it?"

Princess Patch said, "A puppy is in trouble."

Prince BJ said, "We must help."

Princess Patch said, "We will."

Before she could get the words out of her mouth, Prince BJ yelled, "Princess Patch, it's Sophia."

Prince BJ broke down into tears. Princess Patch comforted him and said, "We will help, and the rangers are helping too. She will be fine, so let's go help. We are all suited up."

All of a sudden, strong winds came out of nowhere, and the fire went out of control once again. The puppies were helping the firemen place sandbags around the fire, but they could barely stand; the winds were so strong.

The puppies couldn't help anymore. They could barely stand up. They ran down the path to get away from the heat and grabbed onto a tree to hang on to. Princess Patch said, "I'm scared."

Prince BJ said, "Be brave. This will be over soon."

Then the puppies heard chirping sounds. They looked up, and Lily and Willow came up to the puppies and said, "If your mom could see you now..."

Princess Patch replied, "Yes, she would be mad."

Willow said, "No, she would be proud of you, then she would be mad and take you home." They all laughed.

"Willow and Lily, you must help get Sophia. She needs help. Can you get your friend Ed the Eagle to go in there and pick her up and bring her to us, please?"

"Absolutely! I will be back. Let's see what we can do," said Lily.

When Willow and Lily came back, her friends were following her, and there was Sophia unhurt. Prince BJ said, "Thank you, thank you so much, Ed the Eagle."

Princess Patch asked Sophia, "Are you okay, Sophia?"

She said while coughing a little bit, "I think so."

"I think you should go and get checked out," said Princess Patch. "Prince BJ will go with you."

Sophia turned to Prince BJ and said, "Prince BJ, thank you so much."

Princess Patch decided she better check on the rest of their friends. Ed the Eagle was okay, so Ed and Princess Patch went and searched for Raffy the Rabbit, and finally they found Raffy. He was a little sluggish. Princess Patch had packed some water, so she gave Raffy some cold water, and he felt better.

Princess Patch was searching for Liza the Butterfly; she found her. Liza said, "Over here, Princess Patch. Sniple the Snail needs help getting to her nest away from the fire. She can't move that fast."

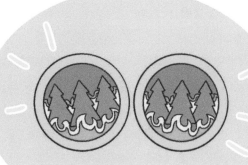

Princess Patch got her friends all taken care of when she remembered the queen's horses. They were in the stables. She told the rangers, "We have to go to the stables where the queen's horses are."

The forest ranger said, "Don't worry, Princess Patch. We have already removed the horses from the stables and taken them to the valley at your cousin's stable."

Then the puppies heard thunder and lightning, and it got closer and closer. The rain started to pour down, and it rained for hours. That was good for the forest; it had put the fire out and saved the trees.

Princess Patch scuffled out of there and back to the tent, and the forest ranger caught up to her, and he said, "I'm bringing you the ranger badges. You two helped do a great thing out there. Make sure Prince BJ gets his ranger badge."

"Ok," said Princess Patch.

Prince BJ and Sophia made it back home, and Sophia was okay. Princess Patch gave Prince BJ his ranger badge. Prince BJ said, "Cool!"

Sophia turned around and said, "Thank you both of you for saving my life." Sophia kissed Prince BJ, and he blushed.

"Wow!" said the puppies. "We can't wait to tell mom."

Princess Patch said, "Speaking of mom, here she comes."

Prince BJ said, "Mom the forest ranger gave us our own ranger badge. Sophia is here. We saved her. She was stuck in the forest fire."

"So I heard. I had a visitor late last night. Here is Sophia's mom."

"Sophia," her mom said. "Sophia."

She wrapped her paws around her so tight and told her, "I was so scared. Prince BJ and Princess Patch saved me. We owe much thanks to them."

"Sophia, you should have never gone out into the forest at night by yourself."

"I know, Mom. I'm sorry. I was trying to find the puppies. They were not in their tent."

"I understand, but you could have got hurt really bad." Sophia apologized to her mom again and reached out to hug everyone with her paws.

Prince BJ said, "Paws up, my family." Everyone giggled.

"Another reason I'm here is that I need to leave town for a business. I'm asking if it would not be any trouble that Sophia could stay for a bit."

Princess Patch turned to Sophia's mom and said, "Absolutely no trouble at all." They all smiled. Prince BJ was in heaven. He was in love with Sophia.

"Are you three okay? Let's get you in the house. How about a cup of hot tea?"

Prince BJ said, "I will take a cold tea, please. Nothing hot for me. Just being in that hot forest last night was enough for me."

"Mom," Princess Patch asked. "Can we put up our tent in our room so all three of us can sleep in it tonight?"

"Why that sounds good," said Mom. "I think it would be wonderful. You guys go ahead and get started putting up the tent. Sophia's mom and I have some things to talk about. We will make you breakfast."

As the pups were walking up the stairs, Prince BJ asked Princess Patch, "When we were coming out of the woods, did you hear someone chopping wood or something going on?"

Princess Patch said, "Oh no! Is this another one of your adventures?"

Prince BJ said, "Maybe." They laughed.

Mom fed them breakfast, and after breakfast, they went to sleep. They were exhausted. They fell asleep on their food. Mom tucked them in. She told them she was very proud of both of them. Well, all of them she was very proud of. She smirked.

Paws up, everyone!

Spread the love

Join us with these tales

About the Author

D. Lindsay is a mother and grandmother who retired from her job five years ago. D. Lindsay always thought of what it would be like to have a dog as a companion. As of this year, the author is a very proud owner of male and female Pekingese puppies. They fill the author's heart with love. D. Lindsay Michelini started writing short stories for her puppies and granddaughter. The author puts all her love and energy into her puppies. These puppies are amazing.

Printed in the USA
CPSIA information can be obtained
at www.ICGtesting.com
LVHW061810250923
758744LV00006B/20

9 798888 515631